Wendel Wandered

Written by Laura Lee Wren
Illustrated by Suzanne Smith

Wendel stood in line at the grocery store
with his mother.

"Stay close to me, Wendel," she said.

Wendel didn't stay close.

Wendel wandered.

He looked at the candy in the next aisle.
"It would be nice to have some gum
and a baseball card," he thought.
But when Wendel looked for his mother,
she was gone!

Wendel didn't worry.

He wandered back and forth,

up and down each aisle,

looking for his mother.

"If I were left alone at the store,"

Wendel wondered,

"would I be put on a shelf

with a price tag stuck on my nose?"

Wendel didn't wonder long.

His mother found him.

Her hands were planted on her hips.

Her mouth scowled.

She did not look happy.

Wendel waited at the airport gate
with his mother.
"Stay close to me, Wendel," she said.
Wendel didn't stay close.
Wendel wandered.

He looked at the baggage
tumbling out of the chute.
He spotted Daddy's black suitcase
with the gray handle.
But when Wendel looked
for his mother, she was gone!

Wendel didn't worry.
He wandered around the circle
at the baggage claim area,
looking for his mother.

"If I were left with the suitcases,"
Wendel wondered,
"would I be sent down the chute?
Would I be put in a plane
and flown to another city?"

Wendel didn't wonder long.

His mother found him.

Her hands were planted on her hips.

Her mouth scowled.

Her eyes glared.

She looked ANGRY.

Wendel waited in the hot-dog line
at the ball game with his mother.

"Stay close to me, Wendel," she said.

Wendel didn't stay close.

Wendel wandered.

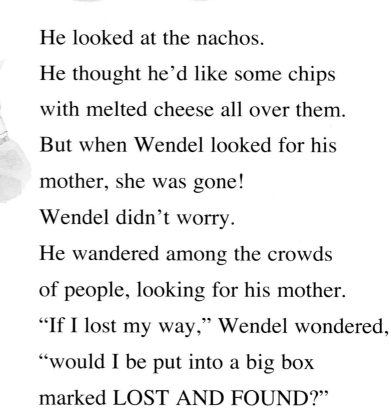

He looked at the nachos.
He thought he'd like some chips
with melted cheese all over them.
But when Wendel looked for his
mother, she was gone!
Wendel didn't worry.
He wandered among the crowds
of people, looking for his mother.
"If I lost my way," Wendel wondered,
"would I be put into a big box
marked LOST AND FOUND?"

Wendel didn't wonder long.

His mother found him.

Her hands were planted on her hips.

Her mouth scowled.

Her eyes glared.

Her face was a deep red.

She looked STEAMED.

Wendel stood in line for the roller coaster
at the fair with his mother.

"Stay close to me, Wendel," she said.

Wendel didn't stay close.

Wendel wandered.

He looked at the giant Ferris wheel.
Riding up high would be more fun
than zooming very fast, he thought.
But when Wendel looked for his mother,
she was gone!

Wendel didn't worry.
He wandered up and down the
snake-like line for the roller
coaster ride, looking for his mother.

"If I got into the wrong line,"
Wendel wondered,
"would I be put on the
giant Ferris wheel to go
around and around forever?"

This time Wendel wondered a long, long time.

Wendel's mother was nowhere to be found.

Wendel waited. Wendel whimpered.

Wendel was worried. Wendel was scared.

Wendel walked to the woman

behind the ticket counter

and whispered, "I'm lost."

Then Wendel found out

what happens to wanderers:

> They don't get put up for sale.

> They don't fly to another city.

> They don't get stuffed into a lost-and-found box.

> They don't sit forever on a Ferris wheel.

> They wait for their mothers.

Wendel waited at the counter.

The woman announced his name over a speaker

so his mother could find him.

Wendel's mother found him.

Her hands reached out.

Her mouth smiled.

A tear formed in her eye.

She looked RELIEVED.

Wendel said he wouldn't wander anymore.